W9-AAV-658

Amelia Bedelia's
• First Field Trip •

That was a long trip
just to see
this field!

By Herman Parish
Pictures by Lynne Avril

Greenwillow Books
An Imprint of HarperCollinsPublishers

Amelia Bedelia's First Field Trip. Text copyright © 2011 by Herman Parish III
Illustrations copyright © 2011 by Lynne Avril
Amelia Bedelia is a registered trademark of Peppermint Partners, LLC.
All rights reserved. Manufactured in China.
For information address HarperCollins Children's Books, a division of HarperCollins Publishers,
10 East 53rd Street, New York, NY 10022. www.harpercollinschildrens.com
Gouache and black pencil were used to prepare the full-color art. The text type is Cantoria MT.
Library of Congress Cataloging-in-Publication Data: Parish, Herman.
Amelia Bedelia's first field trip / by Herman Parish ; illustrated by Lynne Avril. p. cm. "Greenwillow Books."
Summary: Amelia Bedelia goes with her class to visit a farm, where her literal-mindedness causes confusion
along with some laughs.
ISBN 978-0-06-196413-8 (trade bdg.)—ISBN 978-0-06-196414-5 (lib. bdg.)—ISBN 978-0-06-196415-2 (pbk.)
[1. School field trips—Fiction. 2. Farms—Fiction. 3. Humorous stories.] I. Avril, Lynne, (date) ill. II. Title.
PZ7.P2185Ark 2011   [E]—dc22   2010034175
13 14 15 16 17 SCP First Edition 10 9 8 7 6 5 4 3 2.
Greenwillow Books

9/13
E
Parish

For my uncle "Sonny" Dinkins—
a real farmer, a real man—H. P.

For Rose, Catherine, Dick and Diane,
and Ben and our wonderful field trip! —L. A.

Amelia Bedelia was so excited about her class field trip to Fairview Farm!

"We learned about farms in school," said Amelia Bedelia's teacher, Miss Edwards. "And today we're on a real farm with real farmers. Say hello to Mr. and Mrs. Dinkins!"

"Welcome to Fairview Farm," said Mr. Dinkins.
"I'll take you to see the animals, and then Mrs. Dinkins
will show you her garden. She's got a green thumb.
Now, who wants to meet some chickens?"
"We do!" hollered the whole class.

While everyone followed Mr. Dinkins to the chicken coop, Amelia Bedelia stood very still and looked at Mrs. Dinkins. She had never seen a green thumb before, and she wondered which hand it was on. What colors were the other fingers? Did Mrs. Dinkins have a pink pinky?

"Hey, daydreamer!" called Mr. Dinkins.
"Shake a leg!"
Amelia Bedelia looked at her legs.

"Which one?" she asked.
"Which one what?" said Mr. Dinkins.
"You said 'shake a leg,'" said Amelia Bedelia.
"Right," said Mr. Dinkins.

So Amelia Bedelia shook
her right leg and ran to catch up
with her class.

The big rooster perched on top
of the chicken coop was making a racket.
"What a loudmouth!" said Heather
as she covered her ears.
"Roosters don't have mouths,"
said Amelia Bedelia. "He is a loud beak."

Cock·a·doodle·doo!!

"That's Max, and he is our alarm clock," said Mr. Dinkins
    as he poured cracked corn into a feeder. "We go to bed
    with the chickens and wake up with Max."
    Amelia Bedelia was sure glad she didn't have to share
    her bed with chickens or a rooster!

Mr. Dinkins showed everyone how to gather eggs. Some of the eggs were still warm. There were white eggs and brown eggs and speckled eggs and eggs the color of cream.

"Wow," said Holly. "The eggs match the chickens."

Amelia Bedelia discovered an unusual egg. "Look at this one," she said. "The Easter Bunny must have left it."

"Amelia Bedelia, you crack me up," said Clay.

"Uh-oh," said Amelia Bedelia. "I hope I don't do that to the eggs, too."

"Is it true," asked Miss Edwards, "that if a chicken eats something green, like broccoli, she'll lay a green egg?"

Gosh, thought Amelia Bedelia, what if a chicken ate a grape? Or a tomato? Or a candy cane?

"Actually," said Mr. Dinkins, "the color of the eggshell depends on the type of chicken. What they eat makes the yolk lighter or darker. Our hens eat good things, so their yolks are bright yellow like the sun."

The next stop was the dairy barn.
"This is Sunshine, my favorite cow," said Mr. Dinkins.
"Who'd like to milk her?"

Everyone took a turn milking Sunshine. It was tricky work!
"Nice shot, Wade!" said Teddy, laughing.
"Mooooooo!" said Sunshine.

"We have twenty dairy cows, four horses, a herd of goats, and a litter of pigs," said Mr. Dinkins, as he led the class on a tour of the barnyard.

"Look," said Amelia Bedelia. "That baby horse has a ponytail, just like Rose!"

"A baby horse is called a foal," said Miss Edwards. "She's still learning to walk."

"Miss Edwards," said Mr. Dinkins, pointing
at the baby goats. "Do your kids ever
act like *these* kids?"
"They sure do," said Miss Edwards.
"But only at recess."

"Here's our litter," said Mr. Dinkins.
Amelia Bedelia didn't see any
trash—just ten piglets eating.
"Those little piggies went to lunch,"
said Penny.
"So should we," said Mr. Dinkins.

Mrs. Dinkins was waiting for them under an enormous oak tree. She gave each student a chore to do, and soon everyone was helping to get lunch ready.

Angel, Teddy, and Clay wiped down the picnic tables.

Cliff, Daisy, and Dawn swept off the benches.

Wade, Rose, and Heather folded napkins.

Holly, Joy, and Penny filled
the water glasses.

Chip, Skip, and Pat
passed out cheese and bread.

"Hmmm," said Miss Edwards. "Where is Amelia Bedelia?"

"I asked her
to toss the salad,"
said Mrs. Dinkins.
"Oh dear,"
said Miss Edwards.

By the time Miss Edwards found Amelia Bedelia, the salad bowl was empty. "Where did you toss the salad?" asked Miss Edwards.

"I tossed it all over," said Amelia Bedelia.

"Over there.

And over there

and there

and there."

After everyone had worked together to make a new salad,
the class had lunch. Then Mr. and Mrs. Dinkins took them
to the hay barn. They each got to sit on a real tractor. And
they lined up to take turns on the rope swing.
Guess who was brave enough to go first?
"Hey, look out!" said Holly.

"Look out, hay!" shouted Amelia Bedelia,
landing in a big, bouncy pile.

Mr. Dinkins yawned. "I'd like to hit the hay, too," he said.
"Have a quick nap, dear," said Mrs. Dinkins. "We'll go to the garden."

On the way to the garden, Mrs. Dinkins told the class that potatoes sprout eyes, corn has ears, and lettuce grows a head. Her vegetables came to life for Amelia Bedelia.

ShussQuonch!

"What was that?" Chip asked.

Mrs. Dinkins looked at what he had stepped on by mistake.

"That's a squash," she said.

"It is now," said Amelia Bedelia.

"It is totally squashed."

Pinto beans

Navy beans

Wax beans

Rattlesnake beans

Butter beans

While Chip cleaned his shoe, Mrs. Dinkins talked about plants. "We make sure they get plenty of water and sunshine," she said. "This year I planted all sorts of beans—string beans, lima beans, wax beans, scarlet runner beans, soybeans. . . ."

Amelia Bedelia raised her hand. "Do you grow jelly beans?" she asked.

"Well," said Mrs. Dinkins, laughing, "I've never tried to grow a jelly bean, but I'll show you how jelly grows. Follow me."

"Welcome to my berry patch," said Mrs. Dinkins. "Help yourself!
I pick the berries and cook them down for jams and jellies."

As Amelia Bedelia reached for a raspberry, she got snagged on thorns.
When Mrs. Dinkins untangled her, Amelia Bedelia saw her thumbs.
"Mrs. Dinkins," she said, "your thumbs aren't one bit green!"
Mrs. Dinkins smiled. "If you're good at growing things, folks say you
have a green thumb. But you've got to get your hands dirty first."

Getting dirty sounded like great fun to Amelia Bedelia.
"Here, try these blueberries," said Mrs. Dinkins. "But only pick
the blue ones. If a blueberry is red, then it is green. Unripe berries
can give you a tummyache."
How can a berry be blue, red, and green at the same time?
Amelia Bedelia wondered.

"Thank you," she said. "But I prefer
strawberries. When they are red,
they're great!"

It was a long and exciting day at Fairview Farm, but finally
it was time to say good-bye.
"Will the bus be here soon?" asked Amelia Bedelia.
"Actually," said Miss Edwards, "we'll be picked up in car pools."
"Goody," said Amelia Bedelia. "I could use a swim."

"We're mighty glad you came to visit," said Mr. Dinkins. "We have surprise souvenirs for each one of you."

Mrs. Dinkins held out a handful of seeds. "Plant these," she said. "Water them well and give them lots of sunlight. Then one day you'll have pumpkins."

"Pumpkins!" the class yelled. "Hooray for Fairview Farm!"

The next day, Amelia Bedelia's class drew pictures for Mr. and Mrs. Dinkins. Miss Edwards wrote a thank you note and they all signed it. Then they got busy planting their pumpkin seeds.

Everyone got a seed and a cup filled with soil.

"How deep should we plant it?" asked Joy.

"This deep," said Amelia Bedelia, plunging her thumb into the dirt.

She dropped her seed in the hole she'd made and covered it up.

The rest of the class did the same.

"Look," said Amelia Bedelia. "I've got a brown thumb!"
"That's a start," said Miss Edwards. "I'm sure it will turn green in no time!"

And it certainly did.